FIX YOUR OBEDIENCE

7 WAYS TO IDENTIFY AND FIX IT

SWETH 

Clever Fox® PUBLISHING

Chennai • Bangalore

CLEVER FOX PUBLISHING
Chennai, India

Published by CLEVER FOX PUBLISHING 2024
Copyright © Swetha M T 2024

ISBN: 978-93-67079-23-2

CONTENTS

Contents

ABOUT THE AUTHOR

*S*wetha is an Engineer who choose to be a home maker. She chooses to become certified yoga trainer, Podcaster, Influencer. and impart yoga knowledge online. She helped many people achieve wellness in their lives.

She created a podcast called "Just like that", "fit soul & fit body" and "Do You Know?" Listen on Spotify.

She enrolled in MRS Vogue Star and was awarded as Bangalore's "MRS INNOVATIVE." At the Polytechnic College, she worked as a part-time lecturer.

She also believes that self help book can transform everyone's life. She is helping many through her podcast.

She loves to sing and listen to music, travel, and spend time with her family. The purpose of her life is to serve and help the needful.

Let's Follow her on Social Media:

 @swetha_mt

PREFACE

*T*his is for the obedient individuals who are proud of their obedience that they can never make any mistake. This is to inform them that they will realize very late in the long run of their life about little mistakes for which they pay a large price. This can be a Handbook for all those new obedient Individuals.

FOREWORD

Many people fall victim to slavery, also known as Narcissism, under the guise of obedience. There are a few strategies to break free from the naive obedience belief. While obedience has its merits, there will always be others who seek to exploit your advantages or disadvantages.

Obedience is good but on your own terms will be much better.

1

ISOLATING IN THE NAME OF OBEDIENCE

What is Obedience?? What exactly is Obedience? Submission to other people's authority.

The general notion is that obedient people are good. The bad ones aren't obedient.

So, in the name of obedience, these people isolate themselves because they are happy to be known as the good ones.

Here comes the trap. How can you be separated if you are the righteous one? Consider geeks who are first-year college students; they do not want to miss any classes and want to be the teacher's pet. Even lecturers are astounded by such children, and they begin instructing with enthusiasm.

However, in the name of obedience, they will not mix with others. For instance, the entire class does not wish to attend class. Be that as it may, these great ones never need to go along with them. They either need to be in school or return home.

Now, the entire class has concluded that these first benchers won't join any organization and are more concerned with their studies. However, they were unaware that mass bunk would not make them bad. or encourage them to be more reckless. The title of respectful great ones makes them Disconnected from others or say, associates.

Once more " loyal ones" will do nothing that harms their instructor and guardians. But you've been duped; the first piece of advice is to improve your obedience.

Be obedient, but also go out and socialize when the entire class is discussing a topic. Pay attention to your seniors however not at the expense of your needs. Recall you cannot fulfil everybody. Avoid isolating yourself. However, if you're having trouble or discomfort, please try to talk.

Biggest Mistake in isolation is "A thought that people are jealous about you or your obedience".

2

NEVER SAY "NO" ATTITUDE

Whenever you are obedient, everybody takes you for granted. They assume that you will do whatever someone asks you to do. Attention !!! yet again you don't have to accept everyone's request or order. Usually, Obedient people tend to come under peer pressure.

Keep your priorities on the list first. Accept it if and only if you want to do their Job. Don't accept everyone's orders.

2nd tip is to fix your obedience. Obedience toward your work is fine. But taking orders from everyone is not acceptable. You will be occupied by helping other people Work. Work on your priorities. Learn to say "No" politely and never feel any guilt. Unless that is assisting the elderly. Respect and be kind to others. Last but not least, we ought to "give respect and take respect."

conclusion: Learn to say "NO".

"When you say 'yes' to others, make sure you are not saying 'no' to yourself."

– Paulo Coelho

3

EXPECTING OTHERS TO UNDERSTAND INSTEAD OF IGNORING.

What is an Expectation?? Your strong hope or desire that something will happen according to your will or that someone will understand you.

Here comes one more weak point of Obedient people that they expect others to understand. Simple yet complicated. If you want someone to understand you. No!! Just explain to them what you want and what were you thinking.

Assuming things can lead to nowhere. Pay attention to your gut feelings for your objective and you're repairing. Instincts do not always come true in the case of People.

Different people have different thoughts, not necessarily that they understand you automatically.

Quote: EXPECTATION ALWAYS HURTS MAN. Try to ignore if you get mistreated by those who lack understanding.

It's critical to look out for your emotional well-being and yourself.

People behave in any way they choose but remember to ignore them and take good care of yourself.

Possess dignity and self-worth.

Ignorance is the best medicine for arrogance.

4

CLARITY OF LIFE

*S*ometimes we forget exactly what we desire because we are trying to be disciplined and obey. because we are always preoccupied with meeting the demands of others and fail to consider our own needs.

Yet again good that out of peer pressure or in the name of "I find happiness in others happiness is all fake."

As time passes you will eventually drain out. The innocence and excitement that you carry during your childhood will give courage to you to help others as time passes you realize that you need the booster too. And that booster will be injected into you when you take care of your inner child and keep it happy.

And by giving love to your teenage self you will recharge all over again. You will be able to clearly identify what you want out of life, or more accurately, what your mission is, once you learn to love and care for yourself. Confidence in oneself and a clear understanding of your life goals will always make anything you accomplish in life satisfying.

> *"Keep taking time for yourself until you're you again."*

— Lalah Delia

> *"There is you and you. This is a relationship. This is the most important relationship."*

– Nayyirah Waheed

> *"People who lack the clarity, courage, or determination to follow their own dreams will often find ways to discourage yours. Live your truth and don't EVER stop!"*

– Steve Maraboli

> *"When you eliminate the Ego's intense desire to be correct, the clarity of the moment can come through. How simple is that?"*

– Beth Johnson

5

HABIT TO SET YOUR PRIORITIES

*I*n the end, everybody goes in a progression of what you are doing or whatever is happening in your life. As soon as you know precisely what you want or want to accomplish.

Therefore, prioritize

For instance, a large portion of us don't have any idea how to lay out boundaries and they simply need to stream all the others' energy.

How do you determine what your priorities are? Consider whether you, your parents, your girlfriend, or anyone else really matters more than your education. Proceed with your plan even if the person in front of you or the circumstances surrounding them can remain, but your education cannot.

We want to be regret-free when we reach retirement age. I could have bunked and enjoyed, gone out with my crush, chosen to propose to my coworker, and so on. View Being obedient is excellent, but being swayed by peer pressure or the pressure of others is bad. So be sure to prioritize your emotions and feelings over the materialistic stuff around you.

Do you regret previous decisions? Do you have any regrets? Fix them if there are any regrets. Prioritize meeting your EQ before advancing with your IQ. Zeroing the EQ is not a good idea; simply excuse yourself if you do.

6

DON'T LET OTHERS DEFINE YOU

*I*t typically occurs with everyone in your vicinity. People begin to characterize you. while you are working it out on your own. Our upbringing painted a false picture of us Like our parents used to determine who we were. Some people will remain rigid in their character and never wish to change.

Since their parents never stop reminding ·them of who they are. If it is for their benefit or to encourage them, it helps the dejected. If you don't take caution, you could wreck or write someone else's destiny.

We weep while we're babies, but gradually we start to play and grow up. As it is, each of us is a unique individual with the freedom to pursue our dreams.

If you want to get back in shape or gain weight, work on it. Try to heal one another. There is nothing predetermined or written about us. Don't define anyone else.

But having a purpose in life is more important.

Tip to fix it: It is a good one" like you are a good human" Accept it Reject statements such as "You are never good at anything." Whether you want to be good or bad is up to you. But having a purpose in life is far more vital. If they remark, "You've been fat since childhood," don't be discouraged; it simply demonstrates that eating habits are unhealthy. Overall, don't allow someone to humiliate you in the name of "defining you".

Don't let someone else provide you with an answer to a question you have. You ought to find a solution. Go out, spend some quiet time, read some books, and use the Bhagavad Gita. Everything will work itself out.

> *Don't let others define you. Don't let the past confine you. Take charge of your life with confidence and determination and there are no limits on what you can do or be.*
>
> **Michael Josephson**

> *How they treat you defines them. How you treat others defines you.*
>
> **Rita Zahara**

7

WHAT WILL PEOPLE SAY

*H*ow will my parents react? What remarks will my pals make? How will my children respond? Common breaks off all of these ideas.

Whatever others say, there's always your way of doing things. They are unable to see things from your perspective. Put an end to overthinking other people.

Get started on the task you desire. Every person's greatest dread is "What if they are right?" What if they blame me when things go wrong? There's just one way to solve it.

That is, become deaf "if you want to achieve anything in life." Pay attention to your heart. It is always the head that is confused, not the heart.

You'll never be able to explore your fate if you're afraid of being blamed by others.

> *"Care about what other people think and you will always be their prisoner."*
>
> **– Lao Tzu**

> *"Never dull your shine for somebody else."*
>
> **– Tyra Banks**

> *"Doubt kills more dreams than failure ever will. "*
>
> **– Suzy Kassem**

8

PUTTING OTHERS PRIORITIES 1ST FOR APPRECIATION

*T*his is the problem with the majority of the loyal individuals. It is an excellent habit if it is an emergency; otherwise, you are not taking your goals or priorities seriously. Believe me, if you don't take your priorities seriously, your goals will be long gone, leaving you with regret and the expectation of others' appreciation.

You never know what people are thinking; even if your third eye is open and you can feel their positive or negative energy, it is useless. Not everyone shares their emotions. The worst thing you could ever do is study, work, get married, or accomplish any of these things to win the approval of others.

Do not hesitate to put your emotions, objectives, or aspirations first.

Consider other family members' priorities, but don't lose sight of your aim and purpose in life. Take full use of life. All you need to do is justify every emotion you have.

There is no one else who can justify it. Discover and take care of yourself. It's wonderful to be obedient, but not at the expense of your soul's mission.

> *"Decide what you want, decide what you are willing to exchange for it. Establish your priorities and go to work."*
>
> **– H. L. Hunt**

> *Obedience is not measured by our ability to obey laws and principles; obedience is measured by our response to God's voice.*
>
> **– Bill Johnson**

9

FORGETTING YOUR GOAL IN THE NAME OF PERMISSION

*T*his is the ultimate one. Waiting for permission from your elders is acceptable to some level, but waiting till you forget you have desires or objectives is the hardest part.

No matter the circumstances, not everyone can comprehend your viewpoint. Thus, request authorization and bide your time. When they don't understand, inform them and simply go over to find your target.

It is a nice thing to obey. It's a good idea to ask permission. But instead of permitting, they simply want you to complete the assignment. Or maybe they never give a thought to your goal.

Wake up "They are taking advantage of you" It demonstrates your ability. Reach out there. If you are successful, you will be able to demonstrate to them that you walk the talk.

If not it's a lesson for you.

"Awake arise stop not till you reach your goal"

10

TRUSTING YOUR ELDERS INSTEAD OF FINDING YOUR PURPOSE

*T*his is true for the majority of the compliant children. "Believing in your elders rather than comprehending your viewpoint." I am like this, according to my mother. I'm a really good one, according to my father. If someone is defining you positively, that's acceptable.

However, consider If someone close to you says, "You can't survive outside," or "You'll do best at home." Regardless of how they explain things, you pay attention to what they have to say and ultimately reach the same decision.

Explore yourself, take a break, learn about yourself, and believe that you are capable of achieving anything you choose. Except you should have a gut sense about your choice.

You learn from your elders. We learn and grow as a result of how they raise us. However, they can also go wrong. It's not required to accept everything. Trust your instincts and show them that there are various ways to live your life. You have the freedom to live your life on your terms. Additionally, you can **redefine who you are**.

WRAPPING UP

$\mathcal{T}$he 7 steps to overcome obedient mistakes are

1. When you are a regular, obedient student, teacher, employee, parent, spouse, wife, or anything else, try something different whenever someone invites you. It's preferable to give something new a day's trial. Of course, by using every safety measure.

2. Try to use the word "NO" when someone assigns you a lot of work without your approval. Your instincts tell you that you don't want to undertake that extra effort. Then say "NO." Remember, your opinion is crucial to you. Always mind your gut feeling.

3. When your inner self expects someone to comprehend your circumstance, stop thinking about it straight away. Nobody can understand you. So please attempt to explain your situation and degree of pain.

4. Never stop considering your career goals. It's admirable that you're attempting to help and cheer people up. However, keep your future in mind and plan accordingly.

5. Identify your top priorities. While performing your job, your family may occasionally want your assistance. Rather than prioritizing your personal life, you urge your family to be understanding and make the necessary adjustments. This will leave you with lifelong regrets.

   a) Remember your family and your health are your priorities.

   b) Then comes your Goals and your work

6. Never doubt your intuition. Always seek your definition rather than relying on others.

7. Never care about what other people think of you if you are doing something unconventional; instead, follow your gut:

   a) Never expect everyone or anybody in particular to be pleased with your decisions. Anyway, if you're successful, everybody comes to rejoice with you.

   b) Feeling lonely? Thank God if that's the case. Now is the moment to realize who you are. and make the appropriate choice.

It amazes me how many individuals I know have ambitions for where they would like to go in the future yet have no real plan on how they would like to arrive there.

Rather plainly, you're never going to reach your full potential if you carry on with the precise same lifestyle that you are living nowadays. I'm sorry, but someplace along the line, things will have to switch, and you might need to compromise.

ACKNOWLEDGMENTS

*F*irstly, I would like to thank God for giving me the Best Parents, Amazing Spouse and Wonderful Children's.

I would like to dedicate this book to my Mom Suvarna Ediga (Asha Latha), Who was always my charm, my friend and my mentor too.